To: Olivia

FROM: Mom

Christmas 2001

BACH'S BIG ADVENTURE

J.S. BACH

by SALLIE KETCHAM

illustrations by TIMOTHY BUSH

ORCHARD BOOKS   NEW YORK

For my father, Richard Ketcham,
and for his pal Rick
—S.K.

For Walter K.,
friend, colleague, comrade-in-arms
—T.B.

ILLUSTRATOR'S NOTE
The music that appears throughout this book comes from a
piece composed by Jan Adam Reincken.

Text copyright © 1999 by Sallie Ketcham
Illustrations copyright © 1999 by Timothy Bush

Orchard Books, A Grolier Company
95 Madison Avenue
New York, NY 10016

Manufactured in the United States of America
Printed and bound by Phoenix Color Corp.
Book design by Mina Greenstein
The text of this book is set in 12 point Plantin.
The illustrations are watercolor.

1 3 5 7 9 10 8 6 4 2

Library of Congress Cataloging-in-Publication Data
Ketcham, Sallie.
Bach's big adventure / by Sallie Ketcham ; illustrated by Timothy Bush.
p.   cm.
Summary: When young Sebastian Bach learns that old Adam Reincken of Hamburg is
a better organist than himself, he sets out to meet his rival.
ISBN 0-531-30140-0 (trade : alk. paper)—ISBN 0-531-33140-7 (lib. bdg. : alk. paper)
1. Bach, Johann Sebastian, 1685–1750—Juvenile fiction. [1. Bach, Johann Sebastian,
1685–1750—Fiction.   2. Organists—Fiction.]   I. Bush, Timothy, ill.   II. Title.
Pz7.K488Bac   1999   [E]—dc21   98-36111

Like many great composers, Johann Sebastian Bach (1685–1750) came from a musical family. Bach grew up in Thuringia, a quiet province in northern Germany, where several generations of his family had worked as village musicians, singers, and choirmasters. Although Bach quickly won fame as a gifted organist, his father and brother taught him to play a range of instruments. These skills helped Bach to become history's best and most celebrated baroque composer.

In Bach's day, musicians relied on wealthy patrons to sponsor their work. Bach wrote most of his church, choir, and chamber music for the royal courts of Germany. He composed an astonishing amount of music—in part to support his large family. Bach had twenty children, four of whom also became composers.

Bach's Big Adventure is based on a story that Bach liked to tell about his long walk to hear the famous organist, Jan Adam Reincken (1623–1722), play in St. Catherine's Church in Hamburg. Reincken's musical style greatly influenced Bach, who later wrote arrangements for some of Reincken's work. Reincken lived to the age of ninety-nine, long enough to see his friend Bach be acknowledged as the greatest organist in all of Germany and the world.

THE BACH FAMILY was a bit unusual. They named their boys Johann—all of them. They talked of nothing but music and played their trumpets in the street. Still, no one had ever met anyone quite like Johann Sebastian.

Even Sebastian's father, Johann Ambrosius, was astonished at his son's talent. Sebastian played music like a master—by ear, by sight, and by heart. Although the Bachs had very little money, they had great hopes for Sebastian. They dreamed that Sebastian would someday perform before the royal courts of Europe.

JOHANN

SEBASTIAN

JOHANN JAKOB

There are Bach family musicians in my village too. Yes, they are all over Europe.

JOHANN JONAS

JOHANN CHRISTOPH

JOHANN AMBROSIUS

But Sebastian was only ten when his father died, so he went to live with his brother Johann Christoph, a humble choirmaster, in a fairy-tale village near cool, green mountains that echoed with birdsong.

Every morning, Sebastian liked to drown out the birdcalls by playing on the town organ.

"Ouch!" he hollered. "That's my ear!"

"Late again, Sebastian," said his brother Christoph as he hauled the boy off the bench.

Sebastian's secondhand shoes clattered down the church's stone floor. They were so large he had to stuff them with straw.

"Go to school," Christoph said severely. "This instant."

"I AM BACH!"

Sebastian shouted. "I'm through with school. For I am the greatest organist in all of Germany and the world!"

"No," his brother said slowly. "Not exactly."

"What?" Sebastian cried.

"I said you are *not* the greatest organist in all of Germany and the world."

"I am," Sebastian said, and he stamped his foot.

"You are the naughtiest boy in Germany, but you are not the greatest organist."

Christoph put his hands on Sebastian's shoulders and turned him around. "Sebastian," he said, "are you going to spend the rest of your life here with me, playing that old tin whistle of an organ . . . or are you going to study hard, win a music scholarship, and go out and see the world?"

Sebastian thought it over. He didn't want to study Latin, or mathematics, or anything but music. On the other hand, Christoph might actually have a point. So Sebastian started walking—very slowly—toward the school.

"What would Father say?" Christoph muttered sadly, shaking his head.

Sebastian kicked a rock down the narrow street. "He would say that I'm the best!" he called over his shoulder.

Sebastian was so upset he couldn't think straight all day. That night, he wouldn't eat his supper. "Christoph," Sebastian said, "just who is the greatest organist in all the world?"

"Quit worrying, Sebastian," Christoph replied. He patted his brother's head and smiled. "You have rare talent."

"I am the greatest!" Sebastian cried happily.

"Not exactly," said Christoph, chewing his dry bread. "Old Adam Reincken of Hamburg is the best. Go to bed."

Sebastian tossed and turned. He couldn't bear it. He had to know. Christoph kept a copy of Reincken's music locked away in the music cabinet. He wouldn't let Sebastian play it; he said Sebastian wasn't ready. At midnight, Sebastian came up with a plan.

Sebastian tiptoed downstairs. He squeezed his hand between the big brass lock and the bars of the cabinet. Quietly, very carefully, Sebastian rolled the heavy yellow sheets and inched them out. He raced to the window seat and read the notes by moonlight.

Sebastian heard a terrible creaking on the stairs. He jumped, dropped the music, and quickly sat on top of it. Christoph poked his tattered nightcap into the room. "Put it back," he said sternly. "And don't be sneaky."

"It's easy!" Sebastian scoffed. "I could play it with my toes. I'm the best."

"You can't play it like Reincken," his brother sighed, "and you have much to learn."

Sleepwalking! I must be...zzzz.

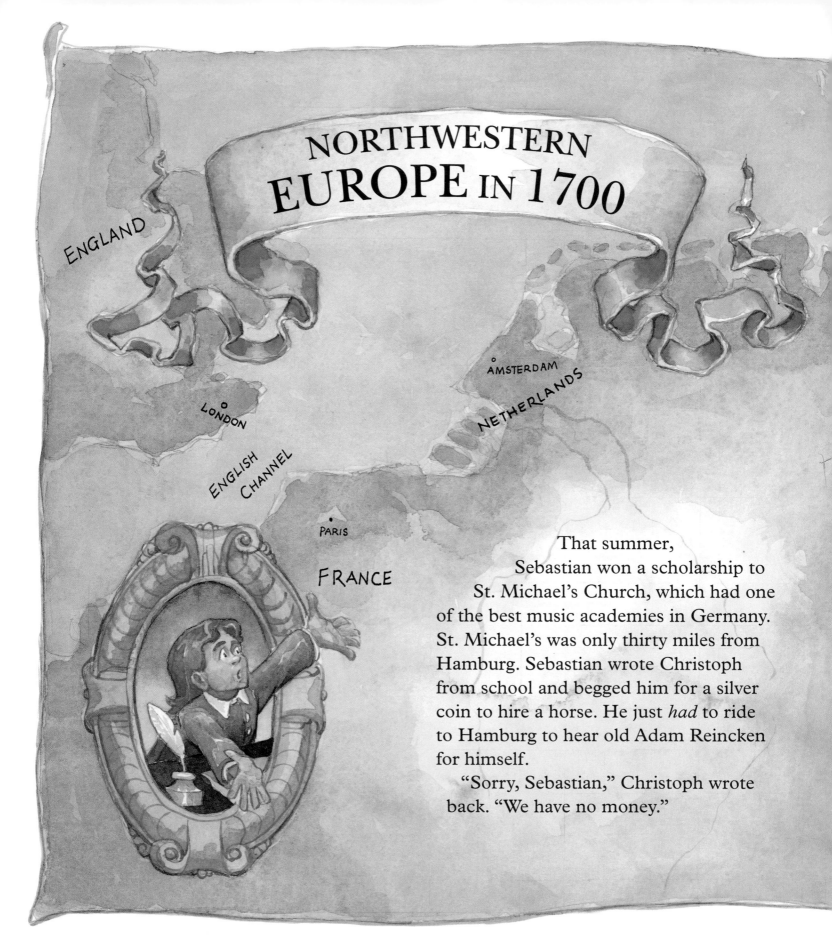

NORTHWESTERN EUROPE IN 1700

ENGLAND

AMSTERDAM

NETHERLANDS

LONDON

ENGLISH CHANNEL

PARIS

FRANCE

That summer, Sebastian won a scholarship to St. Michael's Church, which had one of the best music academies in Germany. St. Michael's was only thirty miles from Hamburg. Sebastian wrote Christoph from school and begged him for a silver coin to hire a horse. He just *had* to ride to Hamburg to hear old Adam Reincken for himself.

"Sorry, Sebastian," Christoph wrote back. "We have no money."

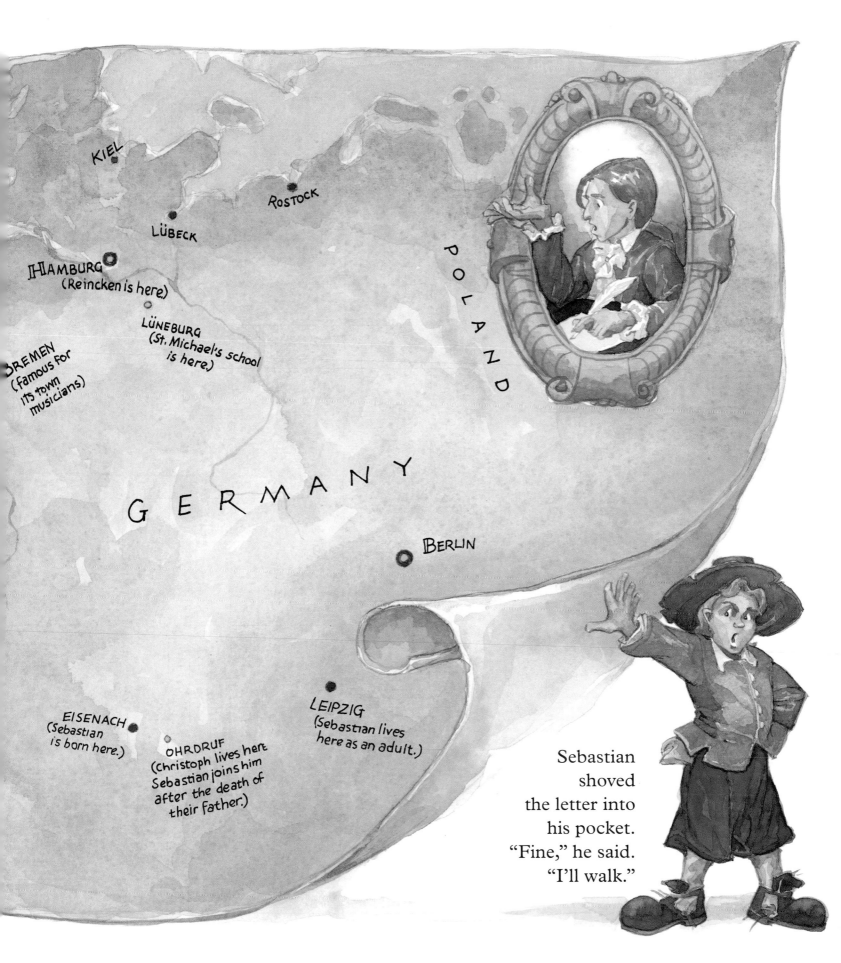

KIEL

ROSTOCK

LÜBECK

HAMBURG
(Reincken is here)

LÜNEBURG
(St. Michael's school
is here.)

BREMEN
(famous for
its town
musicians)

POLAND

GERMANY

BERLIN

EISENACH
(Sebastian
is born here.)

OHRDRUF
(Christoph lives here.
Sebastian joins him
after the death of
their father.)

LEIPZIG
(Sebastian lives
here as an adult.)

Sebastian
shoved
the letter into
his pocket.
"Fine," he said.
"I'll walk."

And walk he did.
He walked away from school.
He put the town behind him, following the
ancient salt-traders' road until he came to a
wind-whipped, rolling heath. He
walked through the wild purple heather
and the golden brown gorse.
He walked past lonely sheep, clinging to
the rocky hillsides. He walked across clear
streams and slipped on the stones.

He walked until he couldn't
walk another step.
  Sebastian stumbled toward a
    half-timbered farmhouse and
slept under the low, thatched eaves
    of the barn. In the morning,
        he stuffed more straw into
            his shoes and kept
                on walking.

By noon, Sebastian was absolutely starving.

He sat on a rock and sniffed the air. Wonderful smells were coming from a nearby inn—sizzling sausages and hot sauerkraut and fresh pumpernickel bread. His stomach gurgled and moaned quite dreadfully.

Sebastian peeked through the kitchen window. "Move along!" shouted the cook.

He peeked again. The angry cook tossed two smelly fish heads right at him! The fish heads bounced off Sebastian and landed in the dirt at his feet.

Sebastian held his nose. He was so hungry and tired and sore he decided to gobble them down. As he picked up one of the stinky fish heads, he heard a funny rattle. He shook the head a bit.

"Herring don't rattle," he said, shaking his supper. Suddenly two small coins rolled out of the fish head. Danish ducats! He could afford to hire a horse, a carriage, and even a pair of footmen!

"A MIRACLE!" Sebastian screamed. He did a little dance under the window.

"I AM BACH!"

he called to the cook. "The greatest organist in all of Germany and the world! Too bad I won't be staying at your inn!"

Sebastian stopped at a dairy near the inn, bought some cheese from the milkmaid, and skipped on to Hamburg.

St. Catherine's Church

Jan Adam Reincken
organist here
1663 - 1722.
Almost sixty years!

When he came to St. Catherine's Church, he crept inside and hid behind a pew. Sebastian's jaw dropped in wonder as he tilted his head, staring up at the most magnificent organ in Germany.

A tiny old man was just sitting down at the organ. His long, white hair was tied back in a bright blue ribbon.

"Ah-ha!" Sebastian whispered, narrowing his eyes. "Reincken."

Reincken's gnarled fingers began to race over the keys—so fast that Sebastian could hardly follow them. Reincken sent his music ringing through the vault of the church.

It soared over the heads of the tired townspeople, who had gathered outside to listen. It soothed the curly sheep, grazing silently on the golden heath. It rolled high above the countryside, dipping with the gulls, until it sailed over the edge of the shining North Sea.

Sebastian gasped. Hot tears stung his eyes and rolled down his cheeks. He sobbed out loud. It couldn't be!

"My goodness!" the old man called. "Who is there?"

"I am Bach!" Sebastian sobbed. "And I used to be the greatest organist in all of Germany and the world!"

"Come here, young Bach," Reincken said kindly. "Play with me."

So Bach and Reincken played together until the sun sank over St. Catherine's steeple in a great wheel of fire.

Sebastian had played his very best for the frail old man. He sat quietly beside Reincken and listened to the evening bells of Hamburg, as they began to peal from all the high old towers of the city, calling the harvesters home. After a long pause, Reincken turned to his new student and said, "I thought the art had died, but now I see it lives in you."

To celebrate, Sebastian spent one of his ducats on a carriage to carry him back to school in style. "After all," he reasoned, "I am Bach. And though I am not the greatest organist in all of Germany and the world . . . one day, I may very well be."

And, one day, he was.